EVIAN RISING

CHAPTER 2 - THE DRAGON'S FANG OF WAR

LATRAVIOUS CALLOWAY

Table of Contents

To my loving family–
Avery, Aryonne, and Erielle

To my awesome supporters on Kickstarter

EVIAN RISING

The Dragon's Fang of War

A Graphic Novel

Latravious Calloway

Vague Sage

CHAPTER 2 - THE DRAGON'S FANG OF WAR

See how it all begins in "Chapter 1 -The Traveling Chaos". Pickup a copy of the ebook, audiobook, and printed version through your favorite distributor's platform.

Visit www.EvianRising.com/shop.

EVEN IF WE DO FINISH UP HERE, FIGHTING THAT DRAGON WOULD BE OUT OF OUR LEAGUE. TEAM MAGNUS IS JUST NOT SETUP TO HANDLE THIS TYPE OF ENEMY. BUT ONE THING IS FOR CERTAIN, IF MAYA CALLS I WILL RISK MY LIFE TO ANSWER. FOR ALL THAT WE HAVE BEEN THROUGH AS A TEAM...

GAH!

WHACK!!

...I KNOW JAXX, CHARLES AND TERRY WOULD SURELY DO THE SAME!

MEANWHILE...

PRAYER FORM!!!

CLAP!!

A PRAYER FORM TECHNIQUE?!?!

HIS ATTACKS ARE RELENTLESS!

HELL FIRE FLARE!!!

FWOOSH

ARGH!

CRACK!

CRACK!

WE NEED TO GET MORE AGGRESSIVE AND TAKE THE ATTACK TO DRIGIN NOW!

WITHOUT A QUESTION WE NEED TO START A LONG RANGE COUNTER OFFENSIVE THEN COMBINE IT WITH SHORT RANGE DISTRACTING CONFRONTATION!

OKAY THEN...IF THAT DRONE'S CANON IS CAPABLE OF DOING SOME DAMAGE, LET IT SHOOT THROUGH THIS WALL AND THEN FOLLOW MY LEAD.

EVIAN IS IT? HERE IS A BIT OF FORESHADOWING FOR YOU, JUST BEFORE I DEVOUR YOUR FLESH TO RESTORE MY OWN.
MAYA, NO...I HAD SO MANY QUESTIONS...
MY CONCEIT. THIS IS WHAT NABIRYE TRIED TO WARN ME OF.
THIS IS THE CONSEQUENCE OF ARROGANCE
THIS ENDS NOW!
PLEASE EXCUSE MY TIMING EVIAN. THE INCANTATIONS NEEDED WERE COMPLEX AND LENGTHY.
EVIAN, HERE IS THE OPENING YOU HAVE BEEN LOOKING FOR!
PRAYER FORM!

AAAHH!!!

I CAN'T CHANNEL ENERGY! MY QI FIELD IS BEING DISRUPTED BY THIS CURSED SPEAR!!

EVIAN, YOU HAVE ANSWERED MY DISTRESSED CALL AND LET ME GUIDE YOU TO MY PLANET NETSIRK. I AM HERE TO BESTOW MY GIFT OF ABONDANCE TO RESTORE AND BALANCE YOUR QI.

ARR!

I CAN FEEL IT... I CAN FEEL MY TRUE POTENTIAL SURGING INSIDE ME!!

SELF FORM!!

IT APPEARS AS THOUGH HE CANNOT MAINTAIN HIS DRAGON TRANSFORMATION.

ARR!!

CRACK!

CRACK!

CRACK!

CRACK!

KABOOM!

YOUR FACE LOOKS MUCH BETTER, NOW MERGED WITH THE PLANET'S TERRAIN. I HOPE THE PAIN FOLLOWS YOU TO THE AFTERLIFE.

ARGH!

I LOST TOTAL MOBILITY IN MY RIGHT ARM FROM THAT FINAL ATTACK.

LOOKS LIKE I HAVE OBVIATED OBLIVION ONCE AGAIN...

IT IS DIFFICULT TO ACCLIMATE TO THE PAIN, BUT AT LEAST I AM AMONG THE LIVING.

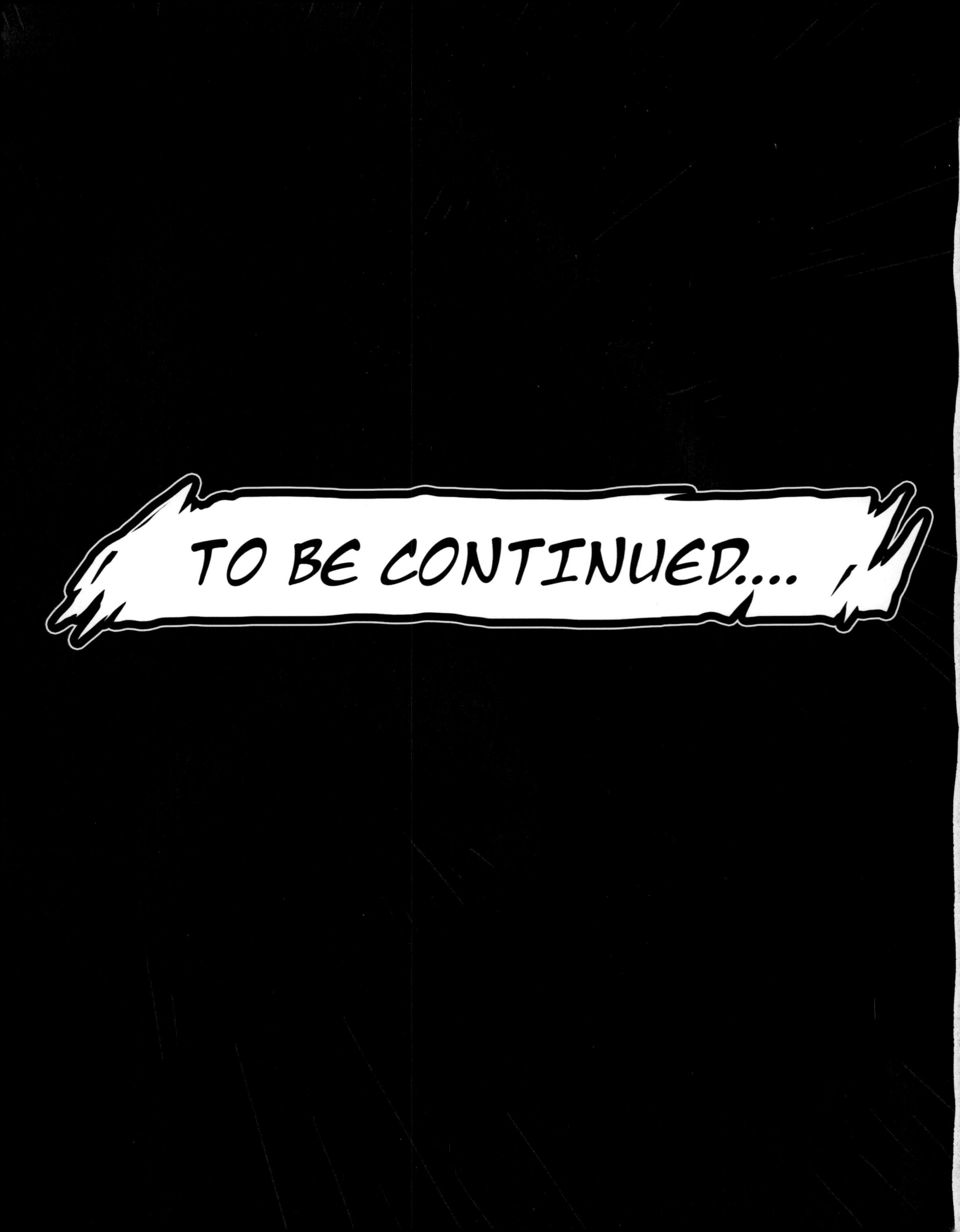
TO BE CONTINUED....

CHIBI CORNER

Maya

Evian

Yohan

EVIAN RISING

The Dragon's Fang of War

A Novel

Latravious Calloway

Vague Sage

Chapter Two

The ground shook beneath Evian and Maya's feet as they stared at the beast in front of them. Maya stood behind Evian in disbelief with her drone in hand.

"Maya, prepare yourself," Evian commanded, as she readied for battle. Her eyes narrowed to focus on this new form of Drigin.

Maya and Drigin met eyes, and Drigin's glare suggested that Evian and Maya were prey before the hunt.

"My heart is pumping like crazy. I can't find the top of my breath," Maya said to herself. Her chest rose and fell increasingly as she witnessed the terrifying sight of Drigin now towering above her. Sweat dripped down her face as she calculated her next moves.

Maya quickly deduced her battle experience was not suited for this style of combat. She felt her mind working double time to recalibrate itself to the situation, activating dormant parts of her brain. Maya was aware of her talents being tailored for working behind the scenes, espionage and gathering intelligence. Just the idea of direct combat had her adrenaline rushing uncontrollably through her body, making her usual keen mental processing go haywire.

"Are you okay?" Evian asked, glancing at Maya out of her peripheral.

"A gigantic monster is staring down at us, deciding who he wants to eat first. Sure, I'm okay. I mean, why wouldn't I be?" Maya said under her breath.

"He's no different from the other enemies you've faced. He can bleed like the two of us can, and I plan to see what color it is." Evian said to Maya.

"Yeah… well, that's the thing. I don't face enemies. I'm the person waiting in the shadows feeding people like you, information about the enemy."

Lips curving in an amused smile, Evian turned her full attention back towards Drigin. "Well, consider today as a coming out party."

Drigin opened his mouth and bellowed a deafening sound causing tremors in the terrain. "Peasants! Witness the incredible aura of a GOD! Mudarar is almighty, and his will cannot be denied. You will be but mere sacrificial lambs on my altar. Tremble in fear from the Dragon's Fang of… WAR!"

The force of his roar blew a gust of wind toward Maya and Evian, and with it came an avalanche of sand and rocks. Reacting to the wind and debris, they immediately guarded their faces. To not lose their balance, they crouched low to find some stability.

"The heat and pressure are immense," Maya said from behind her hand. "I hope all of this is going according to your calculations."

"He's strong," Evian replied, lowering her head, to avoid the debris. "This is going to…"

"Wait." Evian looked around as the dust settled, she quickly realized she underestimated Drigin's speed. "Where did he go? I lost track of him in the debris!"

Maya frantically scanned the area and continued her conversation with herself "Had I realized I would be in this level of a skirmish, I would have brought the 2.0 Dual Rook drones. Judging by the size of the enemy and sheer force of his roar, the Dual Bishop drones would have been another great precaution as well. Wait," she stopped suddenly. "Focus Maya! You're overthinking things!"

"I agree with the second and more deceive Maya," Evian replied, still scanning for any sign of Drigin, but trying to create some sense of comfort for Maya through her sarcastic and dark humor. "Where is he?"

They stood on gaurd and scanned the area around them. Maya tried to stop the pounding of her heart and focus on the battle. Drigin was one of the most formidable enemies she ever faced, and she needed to get herself together. However, meeting Evian was such a momentous occasion, and her presence made it hard to concentrate on the battle. Variables she should be computing, details, and outcomes she should be calculating were coming slowly to her which made it difficult to come up with a strategy.

"I am useless to Evian in this condition," Maya said.

Usually, Maya's calculations derive so quickly, she could pick the best and most decisive action before her opponent has realized they have already lost. Her ability to come up with strategies and battle tactics for counteroffensive were uncanny. Today it is entirely different. The thoughts of this reunion with Evian had Maya second, third and fourth guessing her every move.

"I swear I am actually helpful," she said with a frustrated and embarrassed tone, eyes still scanning the horizon for Drigin. "I just seem..."

Evian interrupted Maya. "You're out of your element, but the bottom line is you need to get in it."

Maya heard a small click and whipped around, only to see rolling rocks. She released a sigh while turning to keep looking for Drigin.

"How could something so large just disappear," Maya said.

Maya could feel Evian's aura and didn't sense any levels of fear from her. "She is confident, just how I remember her. Even in the face of this threat." Maya reflected nervously.

Evian, noticing the anxious energy from Maya said, "fear only exist to kill you in two ways. One way is slow, and you can easily stop it when you want to. But it is also what allows the second death."

Maya nodded, then retaking a deep breath she renewed her focus. Quieting her mind and breathing gave her the intuition to look up. As if reality slowed to half-speed, she gasped. Drigin locked eyes with Maya as he came bolting towards them.

"Above us," Maya shouted, "At his current trajectory, he is going to crash right into us, and judging by his weight and the velocity of the attack, the impact would decimate everything around him, up to a hundred-meter radius." Even as Maya began to gather all the variables from the attack, she still felt as though her body significantly trailed the thousands of thoughts she compiles per second.

"Fall back," Evian screamed, they both leaped backward, and barely escaped the impact. However, the shockwave could not be evaded. Maya and Evian were propelled back several feet, sliding and stumbling a distance before coming to a stop.

"This *will* be exciting." Evian thought to herself anticipating the new challenge.

Maya squinted as she scanned Drigin's biometrics. "Judging by the spike in temperature in Drigin's abdomen, we are going to be in need of countering a massive fire-based attack."

"Instant debriefing could prove useful in battles like these. It seems as though Maya comes with some benefits," Evian thought to herself. "If only she could do more analytics and less of the garbage she can't help but spew, she'll be a real asset in the future."

Maya examined Drigin as he roared from afar. She could feel herself drift into her zone, as her brain's processing power charged to Ultra Critical. This Ultra Critical Qi technique was developed by Maya, which creates separate brain processing segments that can make conscious decisions. She does not have to be cognizant to initiate this technique and this time it also activated autonomously. In this state, everything is clear. The Qi infused into her neurons and synapsis, made them work faster and harder. Giving her mental capabilities far beyond most beings.

Maya pondered if the ease of wielding the technique was a response to the impending threat from Drigin or an expression of needing to impress Evian. It was hard to discern, but Maya wasn't in a position to hash out that paradox.

Evian glanced at Maya and noticed her eyes were no longer a dull brown, now her eye emanated a radiant Fuchsia color like her Qi field. To Evian's surprise, Maya could use Qi to augment her analytical prowess. Evian could not recall James mentioning humans having such control over their brain functions to this level with Qi during his training. Evian's photographic memory did recollect research bulletins on the theory of Quantum Organic processing. It only highlighted the Supreme Empress possessing this level of mental acuity along with a few others on her high counsel. Even then, the capabilities were limited to short bursts and needed to be linked with all on the council.

Despite how great Maya's gift was, Evian knew it was counterintuitive to shout every move to the enemy. It would only be so long before the sensory data got them killed.

"How can I harness Maya's skills and compromise our strategies?" Evian thought.

Evian knew there were ways to invoke someone's fighting spirit. "Of course!" Evian exclaimed. "Maya mentioned she had a 'debt' to repay back in Crimson Ritual."

Evian took note of the determination in Maya's eyes, she confirmed the validity of Maya's resolve.

It was quite simple when Evian thought about it. "Being forced to rely on reflexes and reacting to Drigin's attacks would prolong the battle and put herself in danger. However, with Maya's drive to search for me through the galaxy, there should be enough motivation to not let any harm come to me."

Evian concluded with a smile. "It risky, but…The risk is what makes victories savory."

"Maya," Evian said as she stared at Drigin. "With your heighten awareness matching my true battle focus zone we will have a chance to defeat Drigin for good. This bastard has the audacity to bare his teeth. He obviously doesn't know who I am, but he will know after I stomp a hole in his chest."

"Okay...I mean…Affirmative," Maya nodded. "What do you want me to do?"

Evian announced the plan. "It's simple. You attack Drigin and I will be the diversion. No words necessary. Attack as if I am not present and I will interpret your battle style intuitively."

"So, I'll be the over-soul, and you will be my alluring avatar," Maya said, sounding excited.

"What? Don't make this complicated and concentrate on reality." Evian said. "From the Qi I sense from you, plus your computational prowess, we should be able to overwhelm Drigin. Are you ready?" Evian asked, channeling Qi throughout her body.

Maya nodded her head, gesturing to her drone. "I'm beyond ready!" Maya relaxed, inhaling her deepest breath and finding the concentration she needed.

BLEEP, BERP!

"John Garrison transmission," announced in Maya's ear, startling her.

"A Transmission? Now?" Maya said with confusion.

Evian looked at Maya with annoyance. "What's that?"

"My comm unit," Maya replied. "Why is John contacting me?" Maya thought.

John's voice came through the communication unit. "Maya are you there?"

"Yes, what is it?" Maya shouted.

"A huge dragon burst through the top of Crimson Rituals, and it appears to have headed your way!"

Maya couldn't resist the urge to speak through her teeth. "I'm aware!" She looked up to see Evian disdain. "John focus on the enemies in front of you. I'm ending this transmission."

Evian's gaze pierced the frustration she delivered to John. "Why aren't you taking *your* advice?"

"Right," Maya said turning towards Drigin. Then her eyes widened witnessing flaming balls of liquid heading in their direction.

"He's started his next attack," Evian shouted diving to the ground. The heat was immense making running the next tactic they did not have to discuss.

"We have to take cover out of Drigin's line of attack. We're completely exposed, and he has the aerial advantage," Evian said while sprinting to the side, Maya trailed behind but followed her every move.

Maya scanned the terrain with her optical head-mounted visor "There's a canyon just ahead, it's empty, and we can take cover there."

Drigin watched Evian and Maya run, still launching fireballs in their direction. "Idiots, if you trap yourselves I will surely kill you with my Hellfire!"

In the canyon, Maya spared a few seconds thinking about her team. She supposed they were doing better than she was.

#

John, Charles, and Jaxx stood back to back, staring at the horde of Mudarar devotees surrounding them.

"You're worried about Maya, aren't you?" Jaxx said to John without a glance.

John nodded. "You noticed? She's already encountered the dragon in combat. It hard not to be concerned."

"Don't worry about Maya, you and I both know she can hold her own," Jaxx said, keeping her eyes on the enemy. "We have a mission of our own to handle. Maya the brain and miss Beautiful Chaos will be okay. Do not underestimate the power of femininity!"

"I'm not underestimating them, it's just..." John trailed off.

Charles interjected. "Well...I just hope all the femininity from Crimson Rituals watches this heart-stopping swordplay!"

John replied in disbelief. "Only you would still find a way to brag in this situation. Still, I guess you have a point." He looked around. "Where is Terry? He should be providing backup for us."

Jaxx scoffed. "'Backup?' What the hell do we need 'backup' for?"

"Fair enough...But there is still no excuse for him to abandon us like this," John replied as he scanned for Terry. "Anyone have eyes on Terry?"

"Negative," Charles replied.

"We don't need help for this garbage," Jaxx reiterated. "Besides, you know Terry. He's probably selling surveillance and drone defense services to these locals. Forget him and worry more about the here and now. Plus, this is a big change in the scope of the original mission. So, Maya will owe us quite the hazard pay. That means money for my mech toys."

John shook his head. "Always obsessing over your 'mech toys'. You don't get tired of throwing your money away on machines?"

"Get tired?" Jaxx was taken aback by the mere question. "Hell no. Besides, all this action has my twin pistols raging with excitement. I can feel them pulsating with eagerness to find and annihilate their targets."

Pistols gleaming, Jaxx crossed her wrist and channeled Qi. "Self-form Twin Pistol Waltz!" With a smile, she looked at the creatures in front of her and said. "You think you have an advantage because of your numbers? Taking on multiple targets is my specialty."

Jaxx raised her pistols in the air and with a kick of her foot, she was off. Moving around her targets, spinning, turning, and changing direction so swiftly; her opponents grew disoriented as they fought to keep up with her movements. It was hypnotic the way she moved. Knowing at any moment Jaxx was poised to strike, and the enemy feared their immobility while caught her trance. The more she moved, the more disoriented her targets became, and the more accurate her own shots became.

~ Flashback ~

A time ago, Jaxx excelled in the art of dance while growing up with her family on planet Aura Revel, an intergalactic festival where every day was a new extravaganza. Her mother was a sharpshooter and her father and brothers were seasoned acrobats. Being the natural showman, Jaxx combined those influences and refined her skills to expert precision. After years of pushing her talents to their pinnacle, she was able to surpass the legacy of her family by executing her sharpshooting skills and acrobatics simultaneously.

Jaxx's command of her audience earned her numerous featured acts. However, night after night, and day after day the life of being out in front became tiring.

"I am busting my ass every day and for crumbs," Jaxx thought. "I will give my son the legacy and life I was never promised. I have to make more money for his future."

After one of Jaxx's premiere shows, a woman who had been following Jaxx's entertainment career left a package and message in her dressing room chair.

"More gifts from my adoring fans? If it weren't for you all and my son, I would've quit this business ages ago." Jaxx mentioned to herself as she reached for the digital envelope. However, to her surprise, the gift wasn't from a usual admirer.

"Hello Jaxx,

My name is Ebony Magnus, Director of Recruitment for Askii Operations Corps. I travel the galaxy in search of top talent with unique abilities. I have followed your career for some time now and I think your abilities are extraordinary. I want to extend an offer of placement in Askii's special forces. In the package, you will find a contract for citizenship on planet Askii and more than enough funds to hit the restart button on life.

Come work at a place where your compensation will match your skills. Let's talk soon.

Regards,

Ebony Magnus

Askii Operations Corps

Director of Recruitment"

It was as though Jaxx's prayers were answered, and she never turns down an excellent opportunity. Tired of the monotony of being an entertainer, Jaxx accepted her invitation and gained citizenship on planet Askii. In return, Jaxx gave her services to the planet's black-ops. For a while, the work gave her a chance to bloom into her most refined self, and the rigorous training furthered her skills in Qi manipulation. Jaxx excelled in the art of espionage and weapons design, but that was also not enough to keep her happy. The money was great but the long periods of time away from her son weighed on her heart.

Jaxx could not help but feel the yearning of spending more time with her young son. She knew that developing mechanical weapons was her passion and her son was her number one priority. Jaxx longed to be a part of something that could satisfy both her mind and family. So, she left the special forces and transferred to Maya's intelligence team loving every single moment.

Every night Jaxx was around to tuck her son away to sleep, she thanked the stars for answering her prayers. "Thank you for my son, this new life path, and Team Magnus."

When Jaxx finally wrapped her spell around her targets, she lifted her guns and began to pick off devotees one by one. Yet, her pistols didn't shoot bullets, but sharp blasts of Qi in the shape of needles which she aims at the pain points of her enemies. As soon as her victims are hit, they began to experience pain so intense, it stops their bodies from functioning correctly. If her target is hit enough times, their whole-body system shuts down.

Within moments, dozens of dead bodies lied around her feet.

Charles grinned as he watched Jaxx engage the enemy. "Jaxx is right, enough standing around and gawking. It's time to show the people of Netsirk the power of Team Magnus. Like Jaxx, my weapon is beyond ready to be unsheathed. The spirits of the Nebulan kings are urging me to give them offerings of Qi."

Charles slashed the air with his katana as he went into an offensive position, legs drawn back and blade stretched out. "Sell-form! King One! Nebulan Barrage!" He shouted, charging his katana with Qi. Charles looked up to see the Mudarar devotees staring at him with apprehension and fear. "Come on," he taunted. "Fear won't change the outcome."

When the devotees wouldn't move, he mocked their cowardice with a smile. "Well, if you won't make the first move…" Then Charles dove into the fray, slashing and slicing at his enemies. His katana moving in patterns nearly impossible to follow. Like molten iron through a thin slab of ice, each swing cut his enemies from side to side and end to end.

Charles put his katana away as he stared at the bodies around him. "Nice workout," he nodded his head. Then began to chuckle. "Hazard pay? Now that I think of it, that's funny. Hell, I feel more threatened when I train by myself. Where is the hazard in fighting these spineless cult-following cowards? I should be filleting a dragon right now."

Without aiming, Jaxx lifted the pistol in her left hand and shot the enemy running towards her between the eyes. Three more shots rang out and three more bodies dropped before she turned and pointed a gun in Charles' direction. She shot and watched the energy needle speed past him to bury itself in the throat of a devotee.

"A bit cocky there, Charles?" Jaxx said as she pushed her pistols into their holster.

"Not cocky," he said with a smile as he walked through the bodies on the ground towards her. "I knew you had my back. Besides, I know how much you like a challenge, and I was trying to give you one."

Charles and Jaxx fought alongside each other for years and that made work and banter the norm for most missions. The more complex the job was, the more likely the team would have to engage with the enemy and Team Magnus took the lion share of complex missions.

Jaxx chuckled as they hunted down all the devotees throughout the city. Team Magnus fought long enough to know each other's strengths and weaknesses. They developed from being a group of individuals with unique skills into a high performing unit under Maya's leadership. As a surveillance and reconnaissance team, they were the best on the planet.

The entire squad accepted Maya's obsession with this Evian woman. They knew their leader desperately desired to reconnect with her. For everything Maya selflessly gave to the team, the team pushed themselves to do and earn more for her. The team knew to find Evian, they would need an ultra-deep space vessel. Since these spacecrafts cost a premium, they all willingly took on more lucrative jobs, which also meant more dangerous situations.

Maya was brilliant, and it did not take long for planet Askii to find her as a young girl and help her, help the planet push itself ahead of some of the most advanced civilizations across the galaxy. Maya solved many global issues and invented many technologies. One such invention she patented as a neuro-enhanced web crawler, this ultimate querying technique was so robust, it would multiply itself digitally until it pulls data from everywhere digital information exists. As the web-crawlers comes to decision points in the query it multiples itself to the number of possibilities for each decision. Exploring all potential leads. They also, through the connections of the crawlers, perform real-time fact checking based on all data collected. Even though the web-crawlers were not the most impactful creation she developed, she cherished it as the most precious because this invention gave Maya all the leads she needed to find Evian on planet Netsirk.

John grabbed a creature by the neck, lifted him up and slammed him to the ground vibrating the surrounding area beneath his feet. Then turned just in time to wrap his hands around another one trying to take advantage of his blind side. The scowl he gave was the last thing the devotee saw before he snapped his neck. He turned towards Jaxx and Charles.

"Are you two going to keep blabbing, or help me finish off the rest of these guys?"

"Nah," Jaxx shook her head. "We're good."

"Ha, ha, very funny." John punched another devotee into the wall in front of him. "Even if we do finish up here, it doesn't mean we're ready to take on that dragon. Team Magnus is just not set up to handle that type of enemy."

"Well Maya seems to think with the help of Evian they can take on the dragon," Jaxx said as she stood to her feet. "And I've come to trust her judgment."

"Of course, we all trust her judgment." John slew the last of the devotees with a single punch. "If Maya calls, every one of us would risk our lives to answer."

John walked towards Jaxx and Charles as he thought to himself. "We've been through so much together as a team, and I just hope she is okay."

"I can see you had no restraint projecting your frustration of Maya's situation on the enemy," Jaxx said with a raised brow, gesturing with a slight tip of the head towards the pile of bodies behind John.

John shook his head. "I was simply carrying out my orders, but I could have been thinking about anything while fighting these guys. I wouldn't be so concerned with Maya's fight if I were in a real one."

Charles scoffed. "And here I thought I was the conceited one. Big ego to match a big man? Wait a minute, can someone get a hold of Terry? What the in the hell did he come on this mission for if he isn't going to do the manual work? He's going to be the one cleaning up the bodies. I will not be touching a single corpse, I can promise you all that!"

The three of them stood together and surveyed their handiwork with similar grins of satisfaction.

#

Evian and Maya quickly got to higher ground, breathing heavily from narrowly escaping the canyon where they found cover.

Maya could not help but feel confused and uneasy while in the canyon. Evian relentlessly taunted and provoked Drigin as though she had the advantage. Of all the conventional knowledge Maya acquired, this just seemed counterintuitive. Noticing the peril on Maya's face, Evian quickly explained why she should lose the anxiety.

"Fear only exist to kill you twice." Evian said, "One way is full of distress which creates mental suicide. The other creates an opening for your opponent to kill you the rest of the way."

Maya thought to herself, "She doesn't want me to torture myself with a negative outcome that has yet to be actualized. That is completely logical and illogical at the same time. Everything Evian says and does is like poetry. She is so amazing!" Maya began to take a new posture, gathering confidence as she of all people learned plenty of new things in one day.

It was apparent that Drigin's ego was under assault, and that Evian's words chipped at Drigin's mental acuity. As Evian and Maya stared at Drigin, who didn't seem to be under any threat, felt the pain of being taunted as if he was going to lose the battle. Evian's tongue was razor-sharp and has continuously cut at him since their skirmish at Crimson Rituals. No longer being able to take Evian's verbal assault, he could not hide his fury.

"Enough!" Drigin said as he slammed his claws together. "Prayer-form!"

Maya's eyes widened. "Another spike in temperature in Drigin's abdomen! This fire-based attack will be four point three times as fierce as the last time. There is a zero point zero, two four percent chance of dodging this next attack!" Again, Maya lending her value of real-time quantum data processing.

"A Prayer-form technique?" Evian said. "So, this clown has more tricks I see…"

"Hell Fire Flare!" Drigin discharged an intense flame and immense winds towards Maya and Evian.

Maya clinched her teeth as she witnessed the massive gust of fire approaching them. "There's no way we can evade this one. We're finished!"

Out of Maya's peripheral, she witnessed Evian pulling up an enormous piece of the terrain to shield against the flames. Maya wasted no time and dove behind it while the fire blazed around the makeshift shield. The continuous force was powerful enough to splinter sections of the rock off the sides.

Evian whipped around to face Maya. "If we only defend, sooner or later he is going to land a decisive blow with another unexpected technique. One hit may be all he needs to end this fight. We need to get more aggressive and take the attack to him now before it's too late."

Maya wiped the sweat from her brow and gave a slight nod. "Without question," she replied. "We need to start with a long-range counterstrike. Then combine that with short-range distracting confrontation."

Evian was impressed with how accurately Maya analyzed the Situation. "Okay then, if that drone's cannon is capable of doing some damage, have it shoot through this rock and follow my lead!"

Maya nodded. "Ready!"

Maya took her stance and glanced at Evian, she was flooded with memories of their other life and became inundated by the friendship they used to share.

~ Flashback ~

There she was, Evian, the young aspirant prodigy of the Galactic Federation of Ina. We were all your peers; close in age, but your maturity far exceeded the rest of us. You always seem to have a higher calling, while many were looking to earn only an endowment for their services to the GFI. The beings servicing the GFI were unique and represented Gods from all edges of the galaxy. Most of the deputies in the GFI were young aspirants chartered to bring order, enhance foreign relations and solidify their legacies among the stars.

For me, I often felt insecure about what I wanted from the GFI opportunity; I merely focused on acquiring knowledge and staying to myself.

Maybe it was just a way for me to stay too busy to think about my shortcomings...

But if I wanted to be completely honest with myself...

I just have to admit it...

I mostly stayed busy to keep my mind off being bullied over my shortcomings.

But you...The most regal collection of biological phenomena down to your molecular expression...

Sigh.

After meeting you, I wanted to feel sure about myself. And through the GFI I yearned to make a difference in this world. The frail, short-haired girl with spectacles had a blueprint of confidence, and Evian was the name of this exquisite design.

I will never forget our first in-depth encounter.

"You protected me from them?" said Maya. "Why?" Bruised with her belonging strolled about the GFI's corridor Maya shared a look of bewilderment toward the bold aspirant.

You smiled ever so sarcastically while scanning the scene of bullies scattered throughout the hall. "They're all unconscious, now I have to save all my clever berating for another time."

The aftermath of the skirmish was brutal, but the actual event was satisfyingly over the top. I mean, to see those punks get their proverbial medicine was sensational. However, the sounds their bodies made after being pummeled and contorted almost turned my stomach. Two of the bullies ended up so psychologically damage they renounced their candidacy in the GFI.

You turned towards me with a distinctly different feeling and offered a helpful left hand. I returned a weary right hand as well, all the while processing the recent events. Back on my feet, I was awestruck and couldn't form the words of appreciation. With the awkwardness of silence engulfing me, it made my adrenaline built up to begin frantically picking up my belongs without saying a word.

"Oh no!" I gasped to tame my outburst. "My adrenaline is making the veins in my face dilate…She is going to…She is going to see me blushing!"

"I have to say something, but what?"

"What should I say?" I continued this internal sparring for what seemed to go on forever. Like always, you took perfect care of the curated words released from your lips.

You countered the silence and absence of gratitude with, "The pleasure was all mine."

"Oh no! This undoubtedly is what it feels like when a student fails to carry over enough significant digits for the solution to an equation. My actions were coming off so wrong; she must think I am an ill-mannered cowardly jerk."

Voice cracking, I repeated the question I mention from earlier. "Why did you protect me from them?"

Slightly tilting your head to the side; you released word of profoundness that pierced through my heart from that timeline to the current one.

The concept was so simple but philosophical.

You said "Because it was the right thing to do. How could I call myself defending planets if I decide not to defend one person with the odds against them?"

I took a pause to digest what you said. I heard the words, but all I could think was how right you were. I was going to incarnate wherever Source chooses, and I must be ready to do what is right to help balance the chaotic energy of the planet and usher hope for the inhabitants.

You proceeded to leave the area but not before reassuring me that you are open to being acquaintances. The particular look over your shoulders told me your camaraderie was not necessarily being offered for free.

Then once more, you spoke up with so much candor and directness. "There is a classic strategy game I want to learn. I am sure you will not disappoint me as a teacher. Aren't you ranked highest among all aspirants in this class?"

I remember thinking, "Source of energies in and out of all things living, and private keys to triple encrypted data. This is inconceivable, she already knows who I am?"

The idea that you would, unlike anyone else, care about me no matter what. And in your own way, you made me earn the time spent with you. Because in your heart of hearts you recognized, it was going to take some time to help me build my confidence. More than anything, you knew you had to make significant efforts to make me strong enough to fight on my own.

After telling me I was going to start teaching you chess, you walked off with an expectation. I had to say, even in the short amount of time at that point. I could tell, you did not like wasting time. You were so calculated and powerful, I could only deduce you wanted me to schedule the time for us to meet and to baby step my way into confidence by taking initiative. Brilliant! Your first lesson in authenticity was to be myself and take pride in the things I was good at performing. With just that, it would be natural for me to put forth my best self and I would be able to do it with someone that I admired. And because learning would require multiple interactions, I would incrementally get better with opening up to any person. Especially since I do most things on my own.

~End of Flashback ~

Still lost in her thoughts, Maya continued reflecting. "You were so beautiful; it was hard to keep eye contact."

Maya reflected on Evian training her how to engage in battle. She continued to drift in thought over all the times Evian protected her, and how Evian did so until Maya was able to defend herself. Nevertheless, teaching Evian how to play chess was the most cherished of memories Maya held on to.

"Why are you not focused?" Evian asked without sharing a single glance.

Maya jolted slightly. "I peered into our past-life and felt the physicality of that time and space. I felt the events, I was right there..." Maya's emotions surged as the past-life memories connected to her present awareness.

Maya continued to ramble to Evian, but her words were mostly only coherent to herself. "At a time when you knew me and referred to me as a friend. You may not recall this Evian, but it was you who taught me how to handle intricate celestial weaponry, the one who stood up for me when I couldn't defend myself against our peers in the academy. They sought out to hurt, and humiliate me because they considered me weak and quirky. On the contrary, you showed me how significant I could be. Always calculated and deliberate, you asked me to teach you to play chess. You built my confidence with sustainable terms and set the foundation for who I am today. You were my only confidant, and I will gladly put everything on the line for you."

Maya's sincere words had Evian shuffling through her memory. After a moment of concentration, she was only able to recall snippets of blurry images from which Maya spoke of. Evian tried not to use to much brain power to make the recollection. She was in a life and death situation, and could not squander time dealing with complicated matters. Especially since Evian was unsure how comprehending these flashbacks could help her current or future objectives.

"First things, first Maya!" Evian said, breaking through Maya's dangerous loops of thoughts. "Stop wasting time!" Evian knew Maya could not consciously help being unable to focus, but she needed to be candid to elicit the proper response to the situation.

"Right." Maya assertively responded to Evian as she tilted her chin slightly above a straightforward stare.

As Maya finished her reply, her dormant Qi energy spiked then engulfed her body with a fuschia colored luminous aura. Her energetic field subtly drummed through the air as she formed her unique Self-form technique.

With Maya's revelations stabilizing her confidence, she shouted "Self-form! Rook Drone Release!

The rook drone swiftly unfolded from the heavily reinforced alloy box and latched into its final position. While being controlled by Maya, it made a high-pitched sound indicating that its arm cannon was fully charged. With a smirk, Maya braced herself as she prepared to mentally transmit the fire command to the rook drone. Maya's mental capability for a myriad of advance concepts gave her the perfect aptitude for a Qi powered psychokinesis technique.

"Here we go!" Maya warned as she commanded the rook drone to shoot through the large chunk of terrain shielding both Evian and herself.

The rook drone functioned in two primary ways. It could be enabled in singularity mode, allowing the drone to act on its own accord. Or, the drone could perform like an extension of Maya; manipulating the drone's movements as she serves as the drone's oversoul. She typically gives the drone freewill until she wants it to execute a specific task. Wirelessly powered by Maya's Qi, the drone's vitality is charged and maintained similar to electromagnetic induction coils in wireless docking stations and the devices they charge.

"VEEE!" The drone's cannon drew extra power to overcompensate the force needed to break the boulder Evian held to block the fire. Furthermore, the extra destructive power could counter some of the gust of energy coming toward them.

"KABOOM!" The cannon fired, and the rock splintered into pieces large and small. Meanwhile, Evian used the distraction and resulting dust as cover, springing through the debris and jumping from one falling rock to the other. She was eager to progress to, step two of the counterattack putting direct pressure back on Drigin. The commotion distracted Drigin for just a moment, and he quickly recovered just in time to see Evian coming straight at him. Laughing inwardly, Drigin felt confident this was the end for the blasphemous wench causing him so much trouble. He opened his mouth wide to snap it closed on her.

To Drigin's surprise, Evian used a flash-step technique to swiftly evade the range of his jaws. As though everything was moving in slow motion, Evian's eyes locked with Drigin's and told the ominous nonverbal narrative he now faced. While Drigin's mouth was open, Evian presented a smug look of victory after her and Maya's counteroffensive intuitively progressed. With Drigin distracted by Evian, it made him unaware of his vulnerable state. In the distance, Maya channeled an immense amount of Qi energy to deliver the final blow.

Evian heard the high-pitched sounds of rook drone charging its arm cannon again. Drigin heard that same sound of energy gathering, but it was too late. Maya's rook drone was in the air, aiming its barrel down towards Drigin's open mouth.

"Boom!" A direct hit. The cannon fired down, and the sheer force shook the surrounding area as the energy blast pulverized Drigin and the ground he was standing on. As the drone continued to scorch everything in the path of its beam, the earth cracked under its eminence power and buried him under the wreckage.

Evian stood just at the edge of the crater that had formed above Drigin, an accomplished smile on her face. "Hmph… Maya is actually pretty good. She might be worth keeping around after all. We seem to synchronize so well." She recalled Maya's rambling about their past life. As she thought about it, she did not have to fully communicate their plan for the counteroffensive to harmonize. "Maybe there is some truth to her past life spiel after all."

Maya basked in the spirit of accomplishment after displaying her battle strength. With a confident smile, she proclaimed to Evian. "And that my friend is what I call checkmate." On a roll now, Maya felt witty for tying the references of chess, the instinctual chess strategy they used to take down Drigin and how chess is still a strong bond in which they shared.

"On to the next ass-hole, looks like that will be Disciple 7," Evian said writing off Drigin and getting back to her objective.

She barely finished speaking when laughter thundered from the crater, Drigin laughing as he pushed rocks off him and climbed out of the pit.

Maya became petrified, then immersed with disbelief. "I don't understand, that is impossible!"

Evian grimaced as she stared at the claw at the rim of the crater. "Galactic roaches! These Disciples won't stay dead?" Evian jumped back a couple of feet to shift back to the defensive.

"There is no way he can still be alive," Maya kept saying, fear now merged with the look of surprise on her face. "That was a direct hit, and the drone did not hold back. What kind of monster is this?"

"Evidently the kind that is difficult to kill," Evian replied, trying to calculate her next move.

Then second claw revealed itself as Drigin climbed out of the crater. Even though the shot did not kill him, it was evident that damage was done. The singed odor of alien flesh permeated the battlegrounds as dry winds gusted across the wasteland. Seeing the deep gashes scattered around Drigin's body answered the question of his resilience. However, he still stood self-assured and had more fight in him.

"I must admit, I was impressed the both of you were smart enough to come up with such an attack, and at the same time I'm insulted you would think that such a feeble attack would be able to kill me." He roared, and Maya took a half step back in panic. "A back-rank mate strategy? On the Dragon's Fang of War? I've never been defeated in battle and such basic tactics would never kill me."

Evian knew she needed to put her all into the next attack but using so much Qi at once could permanently damage her body. She stayed laser-focused on Drigin and looked for any signs of openings. Although she felt unphased by Drigin's durability, she knew to win he would have to be defenseless. Reviewing their last tactic made her hesitant to admit that she could create another opening as useful as the first. Nevertheless, she needs to land her most deadly attack, but to do so, Drigin would need to be exposed. The back-rank attack could not kill him when all his defenses were down, so there can be no holding back.

Drigin continued talking. "I must admit, I have to give you both credit for making it this far. But this fight has drawn on for far too long. Time to show you that I have been invariably ahead of you this whole time. I will prove to you the only reason you're still alive is that I willed it so."

Maya looked in bewilderment while Evian quickly took a defensive stance. "This cocky bastard," Evian grumbled to herself

Drigin said with a sinister smile. "See, like the king's gambit tactic, I allowed you think you had the upper hand. When all along I was just exposing my queen to you, so you would leave your back rank open to my attack."

"What?!" Maya said, processing the magnitude of his statement. "That means…"

Suddenly, Maya's peripheral locked on to the subtle movement beneath her. "Drigin must have planted his tail deep in the ground while Evian and I were attacking the interior of his mouth," Maya hypothesized. She was able to recognize Drigin's tail, damaged from the attack on him earlier, ripping through the ground and striking at her.

It was all the time she had, and she knew there was no way she could get out of this one. Frozen in shock, she tried to calculate an escape route and came up with nothing. "Not enough time to evade or get the rook drone to help."

Being out of time was Maya's last thought before Drigin's tail impaled her through her back and out of her stomach.

"Evian!" Maya screamed while choking through the pooled blood in her mouth.

"Maya!!!" Evian responded while witnessing Maya's life leaving her body.

Evian froze in disbelief as Drigin suspended her in the air and let the blood streak down the contours of Maya's Body. Drigin flung Maya near Evian as a taunt giving him time to retract his tail through the ground and back to where he stood.

Drigin bellowed in laughter as he waved his bloody tail against the air. "Evian is it? That is a bit of foreshadowing for you, just before I devour your flesh to restore my own."

"Maya," Evian called silently, "You can't die now, not like this. You were the only link to my memories."

Maya's body lied motionless, and the imagery caused Evian to grit her teeth. The tears in Evian's eyes welled but did not descend. "My conceit. This is what Nabirye tried to warn me about. This is the consequence of my arrogance."

Evian became flooded with emotions she never experienced before. "This is why I work alone, I should have told her to leave. Her life is now on my head."

"Dead men offer no mourning…," Evian thought to herself, remembering the profound remarks of Volker from James's story. The weight of Volker's last words resonated deeper than ever before. And that very statement allowed Evian to regain composure and focus on her overall objective.

She pushed herself to her feet, glancing at Maya "You fought well. Thank you for spending your last moments fighting by my side. Drigin will die by my hands."

Evian causally turned around and pierced Drigin with a menacing expression. "This ends now."

Drigin's sinister laugh toward Evian's reaction vibrated the surrounding area. "Your response is laughable, and while it is empathetic in nature, I would call it simply pathetic. Your predictability and fighting strength are lacking, but it is of no consequence now. It is your time to pay for your sins."

Drigin turned his attention back to Maya, "Your burdensome friend will be delectable." Thinking about the Qi he felt from Maya, he knew she would be quality sustenance to replenish his own and heal his scars. "You know Evian, the final rush of cortisol in your comrade's body will be most exquisite. I will take my time to chew slowly, enjoying the delectable trauma and distress in her blood."

"Enough talk," Evian thought to herself, planted her feet into the ground readying the launch of her next attack. There was a sudden hesitation, Evian intuitively paused as she felt new energy converging in the atmosphere. Drigin, also in tune with the Qi within the area, noticed this shift of power.

"A new pest," Drigin called out as he looked at the sky. "Another pawn trying to enter the battlefield."

The man falling from the sky grimaced as he sensed only two figures watching his descent. Then his disposition intensified realizing there were three beings and the third one is motionless on the ground. Hoping he was not too late, he prepared to make his move.

"Please excuse my timing Evian," the intruder announced echoing across the valley. "The incantations I needed was complex and lengthy."

Evian shaded her eyes to better analyze the man, but he was still too high in the air to make out who he was. She was perplexed by yet another person calling her by name.

Drigin roared, "peasant, you too will be sacrificed to the one that is all high! Mudarar's will is to spread chaos in his name! He has promised me the glory, do you think you can deny my victory?"

Drigin's expression held back zero disdain, pondering the new circumstances. "I will simply slaughter this new ally as another message to Evian. Her will must be crushed before her sacrifice; Mudarar will be pleased with this offering. Maybe he will elevate my Disciple array to number 7. Everyone across the cosmos will kneel before me as I spread the only true doctrine from the almighty Mudarar."

Drigin's thoughts were interrupted as he heard the tones of the intruder's incantation and his eyes widened in disbelief. "He has the ability to channel two Gods at the same time? His spirit should be ripping apart by the sheer complexity of holding two God spirits on a physical plane. How can this be? Who are you?"

The man had no reply as he silenced his mind for the last stage of his technique. His feet slammed to the ground as the velocity met the terrain tossing debris into the air. Simultaneously as his feet touched the ground his hand slapped together in-summons. "Evian, here is the opening you have been looking for. Prayer-form! Light Body Evocation! Conjuring one, Kristen of cosmic-opulence. Conjuring two, Shiva, the destroyer of malevolence."

The stranger slammed his staff against the ground exclaiming the final word of his technique.

There was a sudden distortion in their reality, the sky went dark and static electricity snapped in rapid succession raising the hair on Evian's body. As she assessed the situation, she cautiously held herself against making any move, knowing any rash decision could be dangerous. Furthermore, the newcomer seemed to be on her side.

"This cannot be," Drigin questioned the absurdity of his current circumstance. "I can faintly see two forms. He summoned two Gods!"

The two Gods were almost inanimate as they were composed of a dense light, which gave their bodies a radiant ethereal appearance.

To the mysterious man's right, was the Netsirk Goddess Kristen levitating in the lotus position. Kristen's eyes were closed, as her cape and cowl drifted. The great protector God Shiva stood to the man's left, arms positioned in different formations. Two of Shiva's hands were clasped together while one of the four hands behind him held his divine trident.

Without hesitation, the stranger slammed his palms together and yelled. "TRIS… HU… LA!"

This command awakened Shiva to lift his hand and launch his spear towards Drigin.

Drigin witnessed the trident coming towards him, but it bolted through the air with an unnatural speed. The three-pointed spear pierced Drigin through his chest, lifting him up and sending him back a distance before crashing into the side of a cliff. The valley reverberated in seismic activity.

"Agh!" Drigin groaned placing his claws on the hilt of the spear. "My body, what is this?

The arcs of electricity riddled Drigin's body, causing more pain as he attempted to move.

"What?!" Drigin appeared confused as he struggled with the weapon. "What's happening to me? I can't channel energy. My energy is… My Qi field… is being… disrupted by this… this cursed… spear!"

As Drigin's mouth formed more questions, he visibly got weaker and weaker. Succumbing to the pain, Drigin's claws lost its grip on the spear. The weapon made of ethereal light could not be disturbed through ordinary means. Only through concentration, an individual could touch the spear as it only partially exists in both the physical and ethereal realm. As his body lied defenseless and numb, he was only able to make out the color and shape of individuals on the battlefield.

In the distance, Drigin observed Kristen settling around Evian's physique and for the first time, Drigin's devotion to Mudarar waivered.

Drigin's intuition echoed terrible thoughts of uncertainty, fear, and anxiety. "All is lost. Your reign is over. You are a disgrace to your God Mudarar."

"One moment, I see a man falling from the sky. Then he uses Prayer-form techniques to summon Gods to this world?" Evian thought as she began to feel like Drigin having more questions than answers.

"Stay focus Evian, finish your mission, and get your questions answered by all parties left alive," Evian concluded, not one to let things get her out of her zone.

Evian planted her feet firmly into the terrain and coiled her legs to explode toward Drigin. "Drigin is weakened but do I have enough Qi to deliver a deathblow? If I do not destroy Drigin in this next attack, he could recover, and this battle could end in a stalemate."

Before Evian's legs uncoiled and blazed a trail toward Drigin, she felt something settle around her. The surge of Qi in her body immediately became dense; sharp almost forcing Evian to her knees from its magnitude. The new energy bore no malice or danger. Evian felt the invigorating energy and found herself palms clenched and body postured to slay.

A nonaudible message transmitted to Evian with clarity. "Evian, you have answered my distressed call and let me guide you to my planet Netsirk. I'm here to bestow my gift of abundance to balance and restore your Qi."

Evian could feel one of the two entities around her, like a living armor fueling her and replenish her Qi. "I can feel it… my true potential awakening!" she said, as her voice echoed around the field. "Argh!" Evian exclaimed as Kristen endowed her with Qi. She glanced at Maya lying on the ground. "Your death will not go unavenged," Evian thought to herself, narrowing her focus on Drigin, who stood in the distance struggling with the spear lodged in his chest.

"Self-form!" Evian screamed. "Dark Torrent Cloak!"

A bright aura flashed vividly then transmuted into a dark and rich liquid engulfing her body. Through concentration, Evian carefully titrated the Dark Qi energy into her standard battle Qi field. The ebony colored liquid moved slowly around her skin intensely, but its form still traced her silhouette.

Drigin continued to find trouble moving, but his eyes knew of no such constraint. The dire circumstance of seeing Evian's transformed state walking towards him, had Drigin again, doubting the outcome of the battle. Fear once more creeped in and out of his thoughts as he realized he did not account for and could not counter whatever Evian had in store for him.

"I am Drigin, the eighth Disciple of Mudarar and you're insignificant. Your demise was assured the moment you stepped foot in my province and convinced yourself you could challenge me and live." Drigin called out, desperately trying to talk himself out of what was to come.

Evian maintained a graceful stride towards Drigin, although her Dark Torrent technique tore at her skin and muscle. "Adjust to the pain, step slowly, and stabilize your Qi." Evian recited as she delves deeper into her zone.

All discord from thoughts to pain seemed to stop and then clarity, "The chaos is now tamed, and this will be your end." Evian said. "There are three simple principles which serve as my guiding light, taught by my mother and father…"

As Evian walked forward, the impression from her feet charred the ground. "One; free will is for everyone to use and act upon as they so choose. Two; every being is accountable for their own actions, be it good or bad… positive or negative." She came to a stop, and pebbles and debris began to levitate as Evian went deeper inside of herself to channel the rest of her Qi. The power of her transformation increased in intensity. The pulsating Qi field from Evian's energy vibrated the scales across Drigin's body. "Three; there is always someone out there tasked with making sure no act goes unchecked. And today, I will be your reckoner."

Drigin opened his mouth to give a reply. But it was too late.

"Dark Judgement Fist!" Evian shouted as she stamped one foot on the ground and launched herself through the air towards Drigin.

Evian's first punch into Drigin's throat forced him to swallow his unspoken words. Furthermore, the effect of the dark Qi technique scorched and dissolved the scales around Drigin's neck. The sounds of Drigin's gagging was drowned out by the sounds of a flurry of fierce punches and kicks. Hundreds of punches per second increased to thousands, then to tens of thousands of punches in a focused area until Drigin's inner flesh began to show.

From the way Evian continued to pummel an incapacitated Drigin, it was clear she took this fight more personally than the other Disciples she battled before him.

The interloper continued to monitor the fight with his Incessant Eye gathering and analyzing the now one-sided battle between Evian and Drigin. "Incredible, she was able to knock the dragon into the air with a single punch to his chin. It is clear this cloak makes her movement almost weightless. From the speed of her strikes, and her Dark Torrent Cloak burning every surface it touched, every blow is deadlier than the last.

The mysterious man examined Drigin's mental state from a distance by observing the Qi energy going haywire in Drigin's head. "She must be attacking his mind and body at the same time. Of course, this is similar to what I observed from her through the walls of Crimson Rituals. Once Drigin felt the pain of Evian's fist and made eye contact, her technique must be making him relive all the pain he caused to his victims as they felt in their greatest moments of anguish. And I suppose every hit from her conjures another soul Drigin took. Judging from the way he is screaming in pain it is clear, he lived his life unleashing hell on a myriad of people. What a fearsome technique."

"So, Evian's Dark Judgment Fist not only increases her physical power but when it lands it starts a psychological death simulation. A retribution ability". The stranger was undoubtedly impressed by Evian's skills.

Heat, strength, and unrelenting streams of power emanated violent torrents of dark Qi energy. However, Evian's ability wasn't without its drawbacks and every hit Drigin took, she felt her own type of pain in her body. It was a power that harnessed Qi and turned it into a rolling vortex of energy. The energy was so volatile controlling it would be impossible for most. It took Evian years to develop the skill to combine water and dark Qi release manipulation. Furthermore, for her to wield the power correctly, she needed to stabilize the energy from the technique and prevent it from obliterating her in battle.

Evian knew her technique was not fully mastered, but the pain of not heeding Nabirye's warnings and losing Maya helped to contain the severe adverse effects from the dark cloak. Time was against her, and she knew she would soon have to let go of the transformation or end up mortally damaging herself along with Drigin. She looked up at Drigin, and in a flash, all the events leading to now crossed her mind.

"Fascinating," The stranger commented to himself. "While she has this cloak activated, she can run on top of the water molecules in the air. This must be why she mixes the water Qi energy into the technique; for weightless maneuverability and to meld with the water in the air to be able to step on it."

While in the air, Evian sprinted around Drigin and waited for his body to rise to her at the highest point. Charging her right hand with all the power she could gather from her Dark Torrent Cloak technique, she drew back her now charged fist. Once Drigin was in range, she plunged her knuckles deep inside Drigin's stomach.

At supersonic speed, a loud pop from Evian's velocity, and force echoed through the valley as her fist came down. "I'm the avenger of the Masrurian people and Maya," Evian screamed as she delivered a blow sending Drigin barreling back towards the ground. "Game over you bastard!"

The stranger sensed Drigin's Qi collapse inward on himself. "It appears as though he cannot maintain his dragon transformation. He changed back into his regular body."

Drigin's body blazed like a meteorite, burning hot and bright until hitting the ground. The force formed a crater where he met the terrain and Evian barely landed on her feet just outside of it, kneeling from the fatigue and injuries. Her energy no longer exuded as brilliantly as before and her face once teeming with emotion, now settled back to her usual mask of indifference.

"I feel a dramatic shift in Evian's disposition" The stranger assessed, "it's as though her emotions helped to fuel her last attack and channeled powers she could not access ordinarily."

The remains of Drigin were scattered among the rubble, and his remaining Qi leaked off his body parts. Evian clinched the arm that delivered the killing blow, while pain radiated from it and across the rest of her body. She stared down at Drigin's remains, partly expecting him to emerge again and make a snide remark.

"Seven more Disciples to go," Evian said reviewing her mental kill list "You know Drigin, your face looks much better now, merged with the planet's terrain. And P.S., I hope hell is a place for you on an endless loop of me kicking your ass."

Evian struggled to stand due to fatigue but managed to turn around to walk away from Drigin's final resting place. Grimacing, then falling to a knee, she cautiously attempted to reposition her irresponsive arm. "Argh! I lost mobility in my right arm," she said, agitated about her current vulnerable scenario.

"What in the hell?" An unexpected motion from Evian's peripherals took her by surprise. "Impossible, how did you survive?"

"Looks like I have obviated oblivion once again," Maya said coughing up small pools of blood. "The pain is difficult to acclimate to, but at least I am among the living."

Maya collapsed out of the interior of the rook drone and the outer armor of it dismantled and fell to the ground due to lacking material to hold it together.

"Maya!" Evian called out, pushing herself to her feet trying to make her way to Maya. "You're alive?! But, how?"

Maya looked utterly glazed over while Evian's questions were heard, but her brain slowly processed it. She faintly recollected trying to master her Consciousness Transformation technique for the first time.

~ Flashback ~

"I am done with all of the conjecture, it's time for a real-world test." Maya expressed her tactical analyzer John Garrison, to convince him she was ready to go from theory to application.

"You say this as though everyone has shot their superior in the head. Or shoot any person in the head for that matter." John retorted. "I can't believe I work for a mad scientist."

"I promise I won't die, my calculations are solid," Maya assured John yet again, slowly getting frustrated that she cannot test out her hypothesis.

"Maya, are you hearing yourself? No one on this planet can comprehend your computations." John growled as he crossed his arms. "It's easy for you to say, 'my calculations are solid' since you won't have to live with the guilt if the experiment fails."

"Come on Maya," Charles teased. "You have some balls, I have to give it to you. There is no way I would let my life depend on my math. I'm not that confident. There are some skills best tested as a last resort. You know, in real life and death combat situations. This new technique of yours falls into that category."

Jaxx was in the middle of tightening bolts for her newest mobile suit prototype when she heard Maya and John argue back and forth. The bickering began to drown out the tunes she listens to in order to stay in her focus zone. Tired of their persistent arguing, she turned off her music, stood up, and walked towards them.

"You all have been going on and on about this 'new technique', and I am done pretending that I am able to ignore it. If Maya says she's ready for something then you need to trust her," Jax says walking towards her pistol. "And Charles, never compare a woman's confidence to testicles. 'Balls' are feeble and fragile. A woman can only be compared to something magnificent, powerful, beautiful and mysterious. Like a vagina. There is nothing as strong and resilient like a woman's genitalia. Just to remind you, it can birth other sentient beings, take a thumping and wield an enchanting spell over almost anyone, and anything to name only a few of its rousing superpowers."

Charles snickered, "*touché* Jaxx, I apologize, Maya, you don't 'have some balls' on you. You have some vagina on you."

"Thank you Jaxx." Said Maya.

"Charles your joke lacked complexity, and depth which only solicited a measly smirk. That is negative two points." Maya said eyes still on John.

Maya, John, and Charles all shared a hardy laugh until they realized everyone wasn't laughing.

A small shift in John's eyes told Maya what was going to happen; just before Jax's gun fired.

~ End of Flashback ~

"…I felt the pain from the gunshot, but the body that takes the damage is no longer where my soul resides," Maya finished as she looked up at Evian. "My mind takes something like a 3D image the moment death is imminent and scans it to a nearby drone. I will sum things up to say," - cough – "certain death is avoided as if it never happened. The occurrence happens so swiftly the technique triggers a reflex which makes it impossible for me to die under most circumstances. If I have the Qi energy to execute the technique, a drone," - Ahem – "and a couple of other things.

Consequentially," – cough, sniff – "the pain is very real, and it is something I have not gotten used to. I have only performed this technique three times. And to be fully transparent, one of those times I was testing out my thesis."

"The technique is highly complicated, but I am sure you do not care about the details from previous 'lectures.'" Maya said rushing through her sarcastic conclusion. "Trust me this one, you will make time hear."

The way Evian's brows furrowed Maya knew she did not want to continue standing in the path of her wanting to understand what happened. Maya sighed inwardly as she tried to explain what she meant.

"In quantum-organic processing; a field that I created. There is a scientific principle; which I also created, states that you can essentially upload your consciousness in inanimate objects," - Ahem – "Get this, I reverse engineered my brain, categorized its energy signatures passed the subatomic and quark level. All to develop, what I coined as the 'Soul Code,' modular biological signatures to program the innumerable amount of connections, move my energy identifiers and transmit it via an almost undetectable frequency ledger. The most fascinating part is reconstructing my body composition with the inanimate object. The biotic 3D printing is where the drone plays its role. My drones are all equipped with the right type of elements to put me back together only moments before death, and potentially heal mortal wounds. Any error could be fatal. Therefore, it is best to know the material needed for your vessel. Until I get more proficient at molding elements, I am stuck lugging drones around."

From Maya's explanation, Evian grasped at how Maya managed to survive the killing blow from Drigin but was still shocked at how remarkable her intellectual aptitude was. More than the feeling of astonishment, Evian felt relieved Maya did not die. Nabirye would have haunted her thoughts if Maya expired on her watch, even though she was a stranger to her.

Evian stretched out her left hand to help Maya to her feet once again like Deja vu.

"I'm pleased to see you're still alive," Evian said with a smile.

Maya grinned back as she took Evian's hand and stood to her feet, clutching her midriff. Suddenly, the awareness of the unknown man stood distantly to Evian's rear. They turned around and found him standing at the edge of the hole, looking down at where Drigin's body parts remained.

The stranger gazing into the hole addressed Evian and Maya like long lost friends.

The man spoke without turning around, "Evian, Maya, my two aspirants. Fortune has gifted you two an extension of life and not just from the newly departed threat."

Clarity suddenly descended on Evian and Maya staring at his figure. Evian then took a step forward with caution.

"Master Yohan?" Evian and Maya said simultaneously.

Maya took one more step. "What are you…?"

Yohan turned around pleased with everything he witnessed. "My presence bares two objectives; neutralizing the impending danger from that deceased person's allies. Also, to share my investigation into the conspiracy to assassinate your entire intake class. Thus, disrupting the coalition of deities' incarnation process and putting the universe in peril."

Evian's familiarity of this man and constant lack of environmental control disturbed her. It was as though she was the target of a joke she was not in on. Her fatigued body masked her uneasiness towards the situation. She still had no idea who Maya truly was, and why she felt such a strong need to help her.

"Now this strange man claims to know me, and to top it off," Evian said to herself agitated at the situation. "Maya is experiencing this newcomer with the same faint recollection as me, and I barely know her too. The whole scenario is absurd, and I hate when things are not in order."

Yohan continued talking. "The synchronicity of you two being together and me meeting you all here is fascinating. Maybe it's Source harmonizing this timeline. Most of the beings from your class are dead or have lost their memories. The event which killed so many of your peers had a significant effect on this dimensional time-space. I must help in gathering you all to protect the integrity of Source. I was instructed to gather all aspirants and return to the Director Rona Anagras of the GFI. As the top aspirants of your class, I need you to come with me."

Evian frowned as she stared at Yohan, still trying to figure out how she knew him, and when they may have crossed paths. The more she couldn't remember, the more annoyed she got. "If I hear one more person vaguely explain how they know me, I'm going from frustrated and confused to furious and violent."

Then Evian's gaze went down to Yohan's hands. "What is that obscure thing you're holding?" She asked.

"This is not 'obscure' at all," Yohan replied.

"Are you blind? The dark ball of energy sparking and crackling in your hand. Is that not obscure?" Evian questioned.

"If by blind you mean, devoid of the images generated from the eyes. You are correct. But it is a mere exchange to see with my Incessant Eye." Yohan answered.

"What the hell is an 'Incessant Eye,'" Evian responded "Is that what is on your forehead? Evian continued questioning.

"Still as candid as ever," Yohan said as he grinned to himself.

Maya cut in on the conversation "Yohan, I believe Evian is trying to say is can you elaborate on how this 'Incessant Eye' works?"

"Of course. With my Incessant Eye, I can see and be seen by beings in other dimensions." Yohan continued to elaborate. "My eye has the power to turn my Qi into a beacon, track beings' energy signatures across the cosmos, and channel Gods. The technique serves as a gateway for Gods to manifest themselves and assist if they feel compelled to do so. It was how I summoned Shiva to paralyze Drigin, and then Kristen to replenish your Qi. She mainly wanted to show her appreciation for answering her subtle plea on the way to Netsirk."

Evian's travel to Netsirk came from a lead from Cowin Disciple 12, but more so from the intuition of Evian which synchronized with the distressed Goddess Kristen. It was something that initially astounded Yohan.

"So, to answer your first question, this obscure thing is Drigin's Qi. What is left of it actually, collected and concentrated for you, Evian."

Evian's lips curled in disgust and said "The only thing I wanted from Drigin was a painful death. I accomplished that mission. So, you can keep that."

"I understand you thinking that way. But Evian, you're a gifted balancer with the rare gift to handle unstable energy. You are one among many that can counterbalance its negative essences, and extract Qi to enhance your strength. Consequentially, if you don't take it, the dark energy from the orb could haunt the people of this planet. Which might have a worse effect than leaving Drigin in power on this planet."

There was a skeptical look on Evian's face as she stared at the ball of power in Yohan's hands. Although, she was suspicious of all people her intuition told her that Yohan was telling the truth. She stretched her hand to take possession of the orb, and it began trying to find harmony in her body. There were moments when she felt the urge to throw up, and other moments she was dealt sharp pain through her body. But Evian tolerance for pain was high, and she held composure until it passed.

Evian looked up at Yohan and Maya and said, "Are you all going to keep making my day complicated and painful? I have objectives to complete, and I cannot continue to get delayed."

Yohan smiled as the three of them looked down at Drigin's remains.

#

Evian, Maya, and Yohan headed back to Crimson Ritual exhausted and bruised. Once they stepped inside, you could see petrified patrons, and workers of the club waiting anxiously in quietness. Suddenly the silence was broken when the concerns of the people sounded off from all parts of the room.

"Is it over? What happened? What is going on?" A barrage of questions came shouting throughout the club from different individuals.

"A dead man transformed into a dragon! I have a better question! Why is all of this happening to us? It feels like we've been enslaved here forever." One terrified waiter asked.

The commotion and disorder agitated Evian, so she found the energy to give everyone the answers. "Victims get victimized, in the face of the next tyrant, fight with your all before surrendering your will, and you'll always know exactly what is going on."

The discomfort of Evian's message compelled Maya to redeliver Evian's straightforward message. "You have to be prepared in these hyper anarchic times. Tyrants will seek opportunity and exploit your weaknesses. After going through all of Netsirk's historical data; my conclusion is Mudarar taking over this planet was a purely strategic move to increase his influence. Being an excellent commerce planet; controlling a vital hub of a significant flow of money, resources, people, and ideas stretching across the universe is a no-brainer for pushing sacred doctrine. According to the intelligence, I gathered, many beings from all parts of the galaxy brought their most valuable assets and information for trade. Unbeknownst to travelers, Mudarar sent his eighth Disciple, which you all knew as Drigin. He took no time to rise to power with his might, and his actions short-circuited the activity on the planet. Unsuspecting visitors were captured, put into slavery, or brainwashed to spread the way of Mudarar."

A bartender shouts across the club, "Yeah, and that lady there killed the bastard. The least I can do is submit my free will to help you with your mission. Come on everyone, we owe it to her!"

"Her name is Evian! And I submitted my will to her the moment I laid eyes on that figure." Belle interjected. "My ebony sweet and Beautiful Chaos you returned so quickly, can I express my gratitude yet? I told you am devoted".

Cheers filled the establishment as the will of the people of Netsirk helped deify Evian's persona.

Evian was not used to having an audience, because more than admiration, she cares about her accomplishing her goals. Kill all the Disciples of Mudarar, and then kill Mudarar. No glory, all vengeance.

As Evian continued to suppress the pain from the fight, and Drigin's dark Qi. She began feeling signs of relief from hearing the club's patrons' praises.

Yohan leaned over and whispered to Maya. "Evian is getting a sample worship energy, and among the types of energy you can receive, freewill energy from an individual is the most potent."

"Fascinating," Maya replied. Their free will is literally restoring her Qi and healing her wounds."

Yohan spoke up to ask. "Evian, Maya, will you venture with me to gather the survivors of your class?"

Maya glance at Evian to see her response.

"No," Evian responded. "I have my own mission that I need to see through."

"I thought you would say that, so here is a reasonable proposition for you..." Said Yohan.

Without heat, Evian cut off Yohan, "Be sure to keep it short."

Maya's head whipped towards Yohan.

Yohan smiled and said, "Fair enough, give your word to assist in gathering the GFI aspirants. I will assist you with your mission first. Your opponents will only be stronger. Furthermore, I have never seen a mortal take on a God. You could use my assistance in getting stronger, and my hand in battle. What is your answer?"

Evian paused to assess the risk of taking Yohan up on his offer. "Alright, I will accept your proposal under the conditions that I can modify the terms at any time. For starters, I need a deep space ship for this journey. It should have plenty of room and durability for me to train. Disciple 7 will not be as easy to defeat as the prior Disciples."

Maya chimed in, "If Evian is in, I am in too. I also have just the spacecraft you need."

"Oh, you won't be traveling with me lugging around that monstrosity," Evian said lightheartedly.

"I have been... Well, I was... When it comes to... I have other drones and a technique I need to master... nevermind, I understand." Maya's words and thoughts jumbled, caught off-guard by Evian's candor.

"Well, training for you will also be a priority, because that castle is hardly conspicuous. It looks more absurd than it is noticeable, and I will not have it around me." Evian said directly. "Are you alright?"

"Me? I'm as good as a brand-new quantum battery." Maya replied. "My body is perfect, but the pain is reverberating in my memories causing a feedback loop of agony. But, I will just partition and encrypt a part of my brain in a minute. Then stow the thoughts of those pains into a cold storage compartment never to be reaccessed."

"I hate asking you questions," said Evian.

Maya was slightly embarrassed but internally delighted, Evian in a way confirmed she could stick around with her hero crush and that she cared about her wellbeing. But she needed to ask one more question before she could wholeheartedly dedicate herself to repaying her debts and defend Evian.

"Well, I have a question for you," said Maya. "Why were you instigating the fight with Drigin. It seemed like it made his intent to kill us even more apparent?"

Evian slightly tilted her head in an oblique angle, " battles are more than just brawn, they are psychological. Being awfully intelligent can still lead you to die awfully. If I manage to get you upset, then you are as good as dead. I fight as though I have already won, or that I can defeat them at any stage of the battle. That way it creates no opportunity to think about failure. I also like to demean my opponent to see their facial expressions. There is nothing like making them feel insecure right before taking their lives. Most times, you cannot outsmart insecurities and shortcomings. So, I aim to destroy these bastards' body, mind, and spirit. I want to annihilate every part of my enemy. Therefore, I hope they get livid every time because their rage fuels me to make them madder. They need to know my disdain because I would not want them to die without knowing why. These jerks need to know what it feels like to be helpless before death. Just like, the countless they have affected." Evian replied.

"Oh, I see. Well, you can count on me to protect you with my life. I am eager to show you who I have become. You won't be disappointed." Maya said.

#

...meanwhile in Mudarar's God perspective.

Like being able to pinpoint a person in the collective consciousness. Gods manifest themselves in a separate layer on top of the physical world which houses a plethora of perspectives within the spiritual collective of that layer.

Mudarar's avatar sat as a massive projection on the throne inside his sacred palace. Communicating with the iridescent silhouettes of Evelin - Disciple 7, and six other Disciples, Mudarar conveyed his message through tones and vibrations. "Between spaces not in the physical or ethereal, we meet once more... Evelin, my will wavers in the Netsirk solar system, and Drigin's tributes are waning, just as the Disciples beneath him. Set forth a campaign to take Netsirk and the lower Disciple arrays territories. Sacrifice all Disciples under your array to me and Six could be your new rank. As you undoubtedly know, failure will meet you, your devotees and the peasants that serve them at the precipice of my wrath.

Evelin kneeled in the center of a ritualistic floor sigil, and the remaining six Disciples kneeled behind her. The markings around Evelin's feet served as a mandala or telescope from the physical realm to link to the corresponding God's perspective. In this, case Mudarar.

"Your will is the only way, my lord. I have already taken my leave." Evelin piously replied.

#

Evelin exits her sacred Mudararian shrine and sprawls in her captain's chair.

"Of Course, Drigin was ill prepared to wield the eighth Disciple array. Even though his rank of Disciple 8 is just under my own, there is a vast difference between our powers. Knowing Drigin, he was probably overthrown by peons. But on the contrary, when I come across insignificant peasants. I put them in their place." Evelin exclaimed with disgust.

A fleet of her ships and massive bionic robots traveled through space the headed toward planet Netsirk. "Quiver in fear amongst the presence of Evelin Disciple 7! Your Qi will fuel my mechanical battalion, and there shall be no survivors!" Evelin screamed toward the viewport of her spacecraft from her seat.

#

Maya gathered her team, and debrief them on what happened with Drigin. She went on further to say her goodbyes. "I will be traveling with Evian, and relieving myself as leader of Team Magnus. John will be the new team leader until I figure out my broken memories with Evian. I know it is abrupt, but you all know this is something I have to do. This day has delivered my greatest desire, and I will not avoid my destiny."

Evian's ambition painted a determined look of excitement for things to come. She looked at Yohan, then turn to Maya and said to them both, "it's settled, let's finish this campaign to right some wrongs in this universe."

Evian reflected, "James, Nabyrie, I will avenge your people." Snapping out of her empathetic semblance, she smirked and said to Yohan and Maya. "What do you say we go have a misunderstanding with Disciple 7?"

To be continued…

VAGUE SAGE

Dear Friends,

Thank you for reading, your support, and being a nerd like me. I hope you enjoyed Evian Rising Chapter 2 - The Dragon's Fang of War. I ask that you please be on the lookout for Chapter 3 – Hell's Battalion and the War Among the Stars, Winter 2019.

If you enjoyed chapters 1 and 2, please leave reviews of how much you have loved it everywhere books are distributed online.

 www.EvianRising.com

Thanks again,

Latravious Calloway

Vague Sage

www.EvianRising.com

EVIAN RISING

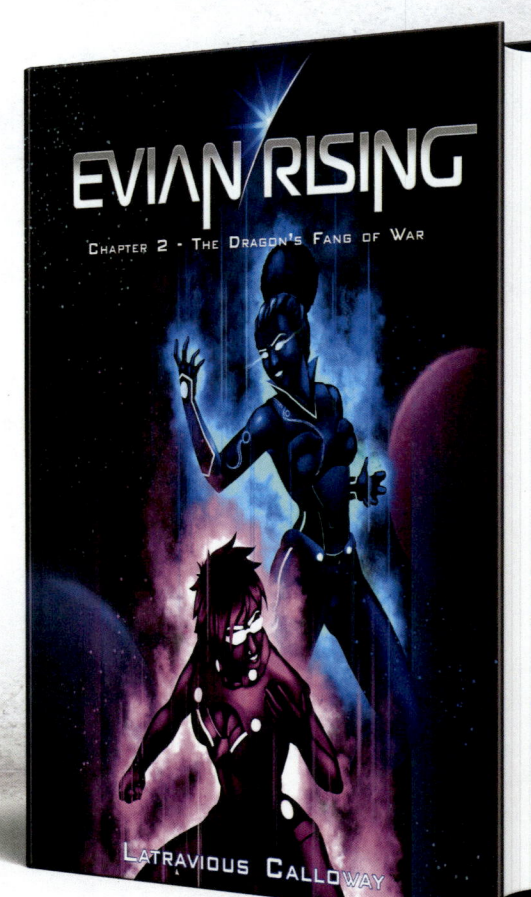

MAYA

43

EV